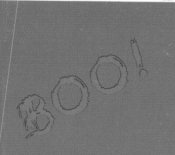
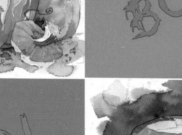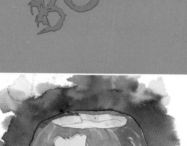
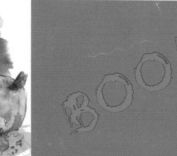
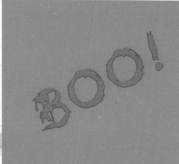

Mick Foley's
HALLOWEEN
HIJINX

with illustrations by
JILL THOMPSON

ReganBooks
An Imprint of HarperCollins Publishers

To Louden, for his second Halloween.
Love, Auntie Jill

FIRST EDITION

Printed on acid-free paper   Don 11/04

Library of Congress Cataloging-in-Publication Data
Foley, Mick.
[Halloween hijinx]
Mick Foley's Halloween hijinx / with illustrations by Jill Thompson.—1st ed.
p. cm.
Summary: A group of monster children and three young humans learn a lesson
about celebrating Halloween from wrestler Mick Foley.
ISBN 0-06-000251-4
[1. Halloween—Fiction. 2. Stories in rhyme.] I. Thompson, Jill, ill. II. Title.
PZ8.3.F698 Mi 2001
[E]—dc21
2001026386

01 02 03 04 05   ❖/WORZ 10 9 8 7 6 5 4 3 2 1

For my three monsters:
Dewey, Noelle,

and Little Mick

The monster children laughed out loud as they put down the book of rules
That was handed out to every child of goblins, ghosts, and ghouls.

These monsters had been good for months, for the rules were very clear:
They were allowed to haunt their forest, but only once a year.

On that one night there were no rules—they could act their very worst.
That night was tomorrow, October thirty-first!

Those monster kids were quite a sight
on the night before Halloween.
A little witch, a tiny wolf, and a boy
whose skin was green.

The green-skinned boy's name was Frank,
his head was large and flat.
It made a perfect resting place
for the witch's tiny cat.

he little witch's name was Why,
the werewolf's name was Where,
Their grandma's name was Wicked,
and their mother's name was Blair.

They loved to scare the human kids—those monsters loved surprises,
But they also gained enjoyment just from seeing kids' disguises.

I love to hear kids cry," said Why. "I love to cause a fuss.
But my favorite part of Halloween is to see kids dressed like us."

That night they slept with ghoulish grins and dreamed about the forest,
And kids disguised as monsters, their screams a frightful chorus.

But meanwhile, as the monster kids
dreamed of screams and scares,
Three best friends on Pumpkin Lane
lay awake with vacant stares.

Lars and Lou and Mia, too, each one in great despair,
Tomorrow would be Halloween, but they had nothing cool to wear.

We could all dress up as monsters," but only seconds after
Lou said those words, he clearly heard the room break out in laughter.

Lars shook his head in disbelief and said, "Monsters are so boring.
Each time I see a wolf or witch I can't keep from snoring."

Just when hope was running low and their cause looked like a lost one,
Lou looked at his wall and saw a poster of Steve Austin.

Of course," yelled Lou with pumping fists as he turned to look at Lars,
"On Halloween we'll all be seen as our favorite Superstars.
You be Steve, I'll be Triple H—the guy they call 'the Game.'
We'll buy a suit of muscles and give Mia Chyna's name."

All three agreed with lightning speed—they knew they would look cool,
They'd buy their favorite costumes when they got off the bus from school.

On Halloween, as evening fell,
  Frank let out a growl.
The moon was up and it was full,
  so Where began to howl.

Why was flying on her broom,
  a thing she did quite often.
"Hee hee," she laughed. "I see some kids.
  Go hide in your coffins!"

Why waited till the time was right, then swooped down and hollered,

"BOO!"

The first kid said, "I'm not scared, and that, my friends, is true."

His colors were red, white, and blue—he wore both stars and spangles. Around his neck he wore some gold, and looked just like Kurt Angle.

here and Frank then reemerged and tried to scare some others
Who carried tables and said, "Whassup!" just like the Dudley brothers.

ot only were the boys not scared, their eyes they never blinked.
"Go get a change of clothes," they said, "those monster costumes stink."

Why and Where just sat and stared as the three kids left the forest. Frank made a vow: "Starting now, kids will not ignore us."

But Frank was wrong, before too long a stream of kids paraded None were scared, they even dared to call the monsters **dated!**

*E*dge and Christian first passed through, then Lita, Kane, and Rock,
And an ugly guy with a leather mask and an old and sweaty sock.

So the little witch cooked up a plan to bring a potion to the store.
She would ruin all the costumes, so they never could be worn.

She checked the index for a hex, inside her book of rules.
And as she did the three best friends were getting home from school.

he children ran straight to the store,
Down the aisle and headed left,
To the costumes of the Superstars of the WF.

*B*ut their favorite costumes were all gone (at least that's what they thought),
   When behind a load of Test costumes that not a single child had bought,

*T*hey saw a lone Stone Cold set and a box of Chyna clothes,
   And one last Triple H costume, complete with rubber nose.

*T*he children smiled big wondrous smiles as they pulled them from the rack.
   Then they heard a booming voice ring out,

"YOU PUT THOSE COSTUMES BACK!"

Why Witch brought forth her bubbling brew and said,
　"Now you'll have to quit.
This spell will make those costumes grow
　and then they'll never fit."

Snarling, Where began to growl;
　he couldn't help but drool.
And Why the witch stepped into
　the small saliva pool.

She completely lost her balance as she cast her wicked spell.
Her pointy hat flew off her head as she skidded, slipped, and

FELL.

The spell whisked by the costume rack—it hooked wide to the right,
Past a Vinnie Mac stand-up, and vanished out of sight!

It came to rest on a tiny box that held a tiny doll,
A likeness of Mick Foley that was only inches tall.

A rugged rumbling soon began, and that tiny action figure
Began to grow and grow and grow and got bigger,

bigger,

BIGGER!

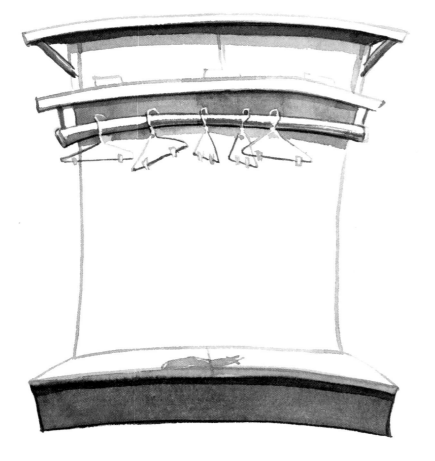

So giant was this Foley doll that Frank's stomach got real weak.
Then the doll just sprang to life and he began to speak.

"You monsters," Foley's voice called out, "should all feel so ashamed.
And you three kids from Pumpkin Lane, you share some of the blame."

Why Witch looked up at Foley's arm and saw her plan unravel;
With a mighty swing the Hardcore King brought down his wooden gavel.

A blinding light then filled the air—Mick had cast a spell.
The store disappeared and the six were trapped inside a giant cell.

I heard your words," Foley said, "and I saw this ugly scene.
I don't think you understand what this evening really means.

When you learn what this night means you all will be set free."
Then before he vanished he said,
"The truth will be your key."

With spirits sinking, they started thinking, and an hour turned into two.
What was the reason for Halloween season?
                              No one had a clue!

Then Where's face began to change, it became a mask of love.
The words he used seemed so enthused as if guided from above:

Mick Foley's trying to tell us to be good to one another.
To Frank I'll be a better friend and to Why a better brother.

It's not about great costumes
        or the time that we spend scaring.
It's nothing you buy in a store;
        no, it means more caring."

Tears ran down his hairy face,
        but Lou seemed quite annoyed—
"Foley is a wrestler,
        he is not Sigmund Freud!

I've read both bestselling books he wrote
        but they are not so deep.
He eats a lot of candy bars
        and then he falls asleep."

*T*hose words from Lou were awful true, there was nothing left to know.
For besides his love of candy and making fun of poor Al Snow,

*M*ick Foley was a simple man, and they all correctly guessed,
Halloween meant tricks or treats and all the candy they could ingest.

A brilliant flash lit the sky and all worries, doubts, and fears
Like the cold steel bars of that great cell

simply disappeared.

They found themselves inside the store and Lou turned quickly to Mia.
"I think I learned my lesson and I have a **great idea.**

I really think the three of us—you and me and Lars—
Should trick-or-treat as monsters instead of Superstars."

The little witch burst out in giggles, Frank and Where both cracked a smile.
They asked the kids from Pumpkin Lane to trade outfits for a while.

The costumes flew high through the air as the kids and monsters switched.
Why wore a suit of Chyna muscles, Mia was a witch.

Flat-headed Frank handed Lou his bolts and his MONSTER CLOTHES
In exchange for Lou's blond Hunter wig and enormous rubber nose.

A leather vest and Stone Cold wig were handed next to Where;
Sadly, Lars then realized the wolf couldn't trade his hair.

For a moment, Halloween seemed doomed, but Lars smiled and yelled,

"LET'S GO!

I'll try acting really dumb so I'll look just like Al Snow."

he candy quest began right then,
    a love for trick-or-treating.
The six friends walked for many miles,
    collecting sweets they would be eating

    heir goody bags began to sag
        and nearly ripped from all the weight,
Until they thought their lower-back discs
    just might herniate.

© Gris h
3·2001

The kids returned to Pumpkin Lane and ate till they felt sick. They enjoyed that special feeling—

thank goodness for old Mick!

Then all six kids **fell fast asleep** as the month turned to November.
HALLOWEEN was done, and it was one **they'd all remember.**

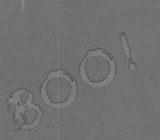